KING ARTHUR
AND THE KNIGHTS OF THE
ROUND TABLE

A GRAPHIC NOVEL

BY M.C. HALL &
C.E. RICHARDS

STONE ARCH BOOKS
A CAPSTONE IMPRINT

Graphic Revolve is published by Stone Arch Books
A Capstone Imprint
1710 Roe Crest Drive, North Mankato, Minnesota 56003
www.capstonepub.com

First published in 2006.

Cataloging-in-Publication Data is available at the Library
of Congress website.
Hardcover ISBN: 978-1-4965-0006-9
Paperback ISBN: 978-1-4965-0025-0

Summary: In a world of wizards, giants, and dragons,
King Arthur and the Knights of the Round Table are the
only defense against the forces of evil that threaten the
kingdom of Camelot.

Common Core back matter written by Dr. Katie Monnin.

Designer: Bob Lentz
Assistant Designer: Peggie Carley
Editor: Donald Lemke
Assistant Editor: Sean Tulien
Creative Director: Heather Kindseth
Editorial Director: Michael Dahl
Publisher: Ashley C. Andersen Zantop

Printed in the United States of America in
Stevens Point, Wisconsin.
052014   008092WZF14

TABLE OF CONTENTS

ABOUT KING ARTHUR

The story of King Arthur is an ancient legend that storytellers passed down for many generations. The story was first told sometime before the 11th century. Finally, in the 15th century, Sir Thomas Malory wrote down his version of these stories. He titled the collection *The Book of King Arthur and His Noble Knights of the Round Table*.

People know little about Malory's interest in the stories of King Arthur. He likely heard different versions of these stories when he was growing up. Perhaps his life experience as a knight helped him better understand the King Arthur stories.

The stories of *King Arthur and the Knights of the Round Table* take place in Britain during the Middle Ages, a time period that lasted from the 5th to the 15th century CE. This was a period of unrest in Britain and Europe as people fought many wars for control of the land. Britain wasn't a united country at the time. Kings and lords throughout what is now England, Wales, and Scotland ruled over small regions scattered across the countryside.

Many people wonder if the legends of King Arthur are real and if the places in the story really existed. Some historians believe that the castle Camelot and the island of Avalon are based on real places in England. For example, some people believe that Arthur is buried beneath the town of Glastonbury. Visitors still travel to England to retrace the supposed steps of King Arthur and his knights.

Merlin

Mordred

Galahad

Long ago, in a dark time, two mighty armies fought.

Uther Pendragon, King of Britain, fought Gorlois, the **Duke** of Cornwall. Uther wanted to marry the **duke**'s beautiful wife, Igraine.

I would give anything to beat my enemy.

Anything, my lord?

Uther Pendragon won the battle. Gorlois was killed, and Igraine became the new Queen of Britain.

Nine months later, a child's cry is heard through the darkness.

And in the darkness, Uther's promise is remembered.

. . . a sword appeared in front of the church.

What does it mean?

Where did it come from?

WHOSOEVER PULLETH THIS SWORD FORTH IS THE TRUE BORN KING OF ALL THE ISLES OF BRITAIN

Whoever pulled the sword from the magic stone would become the King of Britain.

I'll pull it out!

No! I will be the trueborn king!

It's impossible to pull out that sword.

Maybe our king is not here yet.

Oh yes, he is very near.

In another part of the great city . . .

The holiday was also a time for games. Sir Ector and his son, Sir Kay, headed toward the **joust**ing fields. With them was Kay's younger brother, Arthur.

Look at the crowds, father!

A fine knight I am! I've forgotten my sword!

I'll find one, brother!

Where will I find a sword for Kay?

Arthur ran through the dark streets.

I know! I saw a sword in the town square!

Arthur was in too much of a hurry to read the words on the stone.

Arthur hurried back to his father and brother.

It's the sword from the stone!

Sir Kay knew the sword at once. He had already tried to pull it from the stone.

How did you get this, Arthur? We must return to the town square!

Kay needed a sword, Father. I remembered seeing this one. I was only going to borrow it.

People began to gather around the church, and they saw Arthur with the sword from the stone.

By God's will, Arthur is our king!

God save King Arthur!

So the **archbishop** made Arthur a knight and named him king.

The city of Camelot became home to Arthur's court.

CHAPTER X

At one time, King Arthur fought Pellinore, lord of the Ghastly Forest.

KRAK!

Before Pellinore could strike the helpless Arthur, Merlin made Arthur disappear from the battle.

What is happening?

Merlin! Where am I?

Arthur got into the Lady's boat. It took him to the center of the lake.

The boat carried Arthur back to shore. By then, the Lady of the Lake was gone.

Excalibur is mine!

Sir Pellinore rode by them without a glance.

Why does he not speak to us?

My magic is upon him. He cannot see us.

Soon, they returned to Arthur's castle at Camelot.

I shall remember the promise I made to the Lady.

I shall only do good with Excalibur!

Guinevere, the most beautiful woman in the world!

I have brought peace to Britain, Merlin. Shouldn't I marry now?

Is there a lady you fancy?

She is indeed beautiful. Yet I wish you wanted someone else.

She is all I could hope for.

I can see your future, Arthur. This princess shall bring about the end of your kingdom. But I can also see your heart. You truly wish for her.

Good wizard, speak to her father for me.

As you command, my king.

At the castle of King Leodegrance . . .

King Arthur asks to marry your daughter, sire.

He is a noble king. My land shall be his as shall my knights.

And your daughter?

I share my father's high opinion of Arthur. I shall be honored to be his queen.

A wedding date was set.

Guinevere's father sent a huge round table as a wedding gift.

Since this table has no head or foot, every knight is equal.

But why is that seat empty?

I shall sit here!

NOOOOOO!!!!

What's happening?

AHH!

An eager young knight reached for the mysterious chair . . .

The poor knight's skeleton crashed to the floor.

They found the **fortress** of Melwas, surrounded by a **moat** of swords.

This is wizard's magic!

If only Merlin were here.

One brave knight, Lancelot, stepped forward.

The queen's life is at stake!

Lancelot leaped across the **moat**.

KLANG!

Lancelot!

Lancelot became one of Arthur's most trusted knights and his best friend.

Lancelot also loved Guinevere, and the queen silently returned his love.

One day, a strange **hermit** appeared in Camelot.

Come share our meal, old father.

I speak of danger. A princess is kept in a tower by magic.

Only the bravest of knights can save her.

I will go!

38

ROAAAR!

ZZAK!

I owe you my life, sir knight!

Lancelot realized he had been tricked by Pelles and his daughter.

He also knew Guinevere would be angry to hear he was wed, because she loved him.

He felt ashamed. So he rode off into a deep forest, far away from Camelot.

In good time, Elaine's son was born. She named him Galahad and raised him in a faraway castle among wise men and women.

Many years passed. Lancelot became a wild knight of the woods.

Arthur's knights passed through many adventures as they searched for the Holy Grail.

Finally, three of Arthur's knights — Galahad, Percival, and Bors — came to a ruined castle.

Look! It is Lancelot.

Galahad drank from the cup, and then . . .

Galahad and the Grail were never seen again.

His fellow knights returned to Camelot without him.

Soon the whispers reached Arthur. He had no choice but to send Guinevere away.

When Lancelot heard the news, he left Camelot as well.

Arthur was alone. And Mordred continued to plot in the shadows.

Arthur is weak. Join me, and we will rule Britain.

Mordred did his evil work well. Soon he had gathered an army.

Arthur knew a great battle was coming.

Ah, Guinevere and Lancelot. The two people I loved most are gone. And so I fight alone.

The price of battle was high.

That night, Arthur dreamed . . .

Merlin, Merlin, where are you?

It was not Merlin but Galahad who appeared in a vision.

Do not fight this day, Arthur. Make peace with Mordred. In a month, Lancelot will come to help you.

Suddenly, Arthur awoke.

The next morning, Arthur made his plans.

Take this to Mordred. Offer him a portion of my land. We must have peace.

Yes, my lord.

The two sides prepared to meet.

If anyone draws his sword, kill Mordred at once. I do not trust him.

If anyone draws his sword, kill them all!

Arthur and Mordred came to an agreement.

There would be peace after all.

HISS!

SSSSSSS!

By dark, the field was covered with bodies.

My noble knights! So many lost!

At the same time, inside Arthur's castle . . .

The Round Table!

It is splitting apart!

From his vantage point, Arthur saw Mordred.

Traitor! You shall pay!

ABOUT THE RETELLING AUTHOR AND ILLUSTRATOR

M.C. Hall has written more than 80 fiction and nonfiction books for children, including science books, biographies, and fairy tales. She likes to read, walk on the beach, garden, and ski. She lives in the Boston area.

C. E. Richards grew up reading comic books, C. S. Lewis, J. R. R. Tolkien, and watching *Star Wars*. He is a graduate of Savannah College of Art and lives in Atlanta, where he is working on book and magazine illustrations, comic books, poster design, playbill illustration, and album artwork for CDs.

GLOSSARY

archbishop (arch-BISH-up)—the ruler of bishops in some Christian religions

duke (DOOK)—in Britain, a ruler ranked lower than a prince

fortress (FOR-truhss)—a group of buildings protected by walls and forts

hermit (HUR-mit)—a person who lives alone and away from others

joust (JOWST)—a battle with lances or spears fought between knights on horseback

moat (MOHT)—a deep, wide ditch filled with water that surrounds a castle or fortress and keeps people away

perilous (PARE-uhl-uhss)—dangerous

potion (PO-shuhn)—a drink with special powers

prophecy (PROF-uh-see)—a foretelling or prediction of what is going to happen

scabbard (SKAB-urd)—a case that people wear to hold a sword

COMMON CORE ALIGNED
READING QUESTIONS

1. Write down what you know about any of the following topics that are key to this story: knights, wizards, chivalry, kings and queens, love, and battles. Have you read any other stories that use those words? Which stories? Have you ever heard any of these words before? Where and how were they used? *("By the end of the year, read and comprehend literature . . . with scaffolding as needed at the high end of the range.")*

2. Who is Lady Guinevere? Why she is important to the story? *("Describe in depth a character, setting, or event in a story.")*

3. Relationships are important to this story. What evidence in this graphic novel, especially between the characters, would lead you to think that relationships are important? *("Determine a theme of a story.")*

4. Describe Merlin. What is he like? What does he do in the story? Cite specific details in the art and text. *("Describe in depth a character . . . drawing on specific details in the text.")*

5. How does Galahad end up at the Round Table? How do Arthur and the other characters know he belongs at the famous table? *("Refer to details and examples in a text when explaining what the text says explicitly and when drawing inferences from the text.")*

COMMON CORE ALIGNED
WRITING QUESTIONS

1. Who do you think is the strongest character in the story? With evidence from the text write a one-page argument to support your choice. *("Draw evidence from literary . . . texts to support analysis.")*

2. Merlin is often mysterious and magical. If he were to visit you, what magical power would you want him to teach you? Write a one-page answer that identifies which power you would want Merlin to give you, and at least three reasons why. *("Write opinion pieces on topics or texts, supporting a point of view with reasons and information.")*

3. Choose one of your favorite characters from *King Arthur and the Knights of the Round Table* and write a new chapter to the graphic novel. Which character would you be, and what would your chapter be about? Be sure to start your new chapter where the graphic novel ends. *("Write informative/explanatory texts to examine a topic and convey ideas.")*

4. If you could be a knight of the Round Table, what kind of knight would you be? All of the knights in the story are known for a specific value or virtue (for example, Sir Galahad is known for being pure of heart). What would you be known for? Write a two-page creative story about yourself as a new knight of the Round Table. *("Write narratives to develop real or imagined experiences or events.")*

5. Pretend you are a news reporter and write a blog or online news report that explains the legendary quest for the Holy Grail. Why are they searching for the Grail? What kind of adventures do they go on? What happens during their adventures? *("Draw evidence from literary . . . texts to support analysis.")*

READ THEM ALL!

JULES VERNE'S
20,000 LEAGUES UNDER THE SEA
A GRAPHIC NOVEL

MARK TWAIN'S
THE ADVENTURES OF TOM SAWYER
A GRAPHIC NOVEL

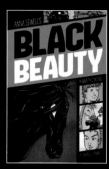
ANNA SEWELL'S
BLACK BEAUTY
A GRAPHIC NOVEL

VICTOR HUGO'S
THE HUNCHBACK OF NOTRE DAME
A GRAPHIC NOVEL

ROBIN HOOD
A GRAPHIC NOVEL

ROBERT LOUIS STEVENSON'S
TREASURE ISLAND
A GRAPHIC NOVEL

MARY SHELLEY'S
FRANKENSTEIN
A GRAPHIC NOVEL

JULES VERNE'S
JOURNEY TO THE CENTER OF THE EARTH
A GRAPHIC NOVEL

ROBERT LOUIS STEVENSON'S
THE STRANGE CASE OF DR. JEKYLL AND MR. HYDE
A GRAPHIC NOVEL
BY BOWEN & FERRAN

WASHINGTON IRVING'S
THE LEGEND OF SLEEPY HOLLOW
A GRAPHIC NOVEL

BRAM STOKER'S
DRACULA

JONATHAN SWIFT'S
GULLIVER'S TRAVELS
A GRAPHIC NOVEL

ARTHUR CONAN DOYLE'S
THE HOUND OF THE BASKERVILLES
A GRAPHIC NOVEL

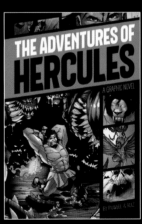